Little Mouse's Trail Tale

Written by JoAnn Vandine
Illustrated by John Burge and Laurie Sharpe

MONDO

This edition first published in the United States of America in 1994 by

MONDO Publishing

By arrangement with MULTIMEDIA INTERNATIONAL (UK) LTD

Printed in China
August, 2012, Prosperous Offset (Shenzhen), 11805
First Mondo printing, October 1994
13 14 15   PB   15 14 13 12

Originally published in Australia in 1989 by Horwitz Publications Pty Ltd
Original development by Robert Andersen & Associates and Snowball Educational

Library of Congress Cataloging-in-Publication Data
Vandine, JoAnn.
    Little mouse's trail tale / written by JoAnn Vandine ; illustrated by John Burge
and Laurie Sharpe.
        p.   cm.
    Summary: One dark night a little mouse follows a trail to a trap, but later a
note leads him to a newfound friend. Accompanied by a die-cut mouse to move
along the dotted trail.
    ISBN 1-879531-59-3 : $4.95
    1. Toy and movable books—Specimens. [1. Mice—Fiction. 2. Stories in
rhyme. 3. Toy and movable books.] I. Burge, John, ill. II. Sharpe, Laurie, ill.
III. Title.
PZ8.3.V37Li   1994
[E]—dc20
                                                    94-30181
                                                      CIP
                                                      AC

A little gray mouse
Got hungry one night
And set out to look
For a tasty bite.

3

He always followed
The very same trail,
Though the night was dark
And the moon was pale.

Through the tunnel,
Over the bridge,
Up the mountain
By the fridge.

Into the cupboard
To look all around,
He smelled something good
And quickly found …

a piece of cake!

Again the next night
He followed the trail.
He knew the long path;
There was no way to fail.

Through the tunnel,
Over the bridge,
Up the mountain
By the fridge.

Into the cupboard
To look all around,
He smelled something good
And quickly found ...

a slice of bread!

Night after night
He followed his plan,
And ate as much food
As a little mouse can.

10

And then one dark night
He set out to feast
On cheese, or cake, or
Small crumbs, at least.

Through the tunnel,
Over the bridge,
Up the mountain
By the fridge.

Into the cupboard
To look all around,
He smelled something good
And quickly found ...

a mousetrap!

13

Out of the cupboard
By the fridge,
Down the mountain,
Over the bridge.

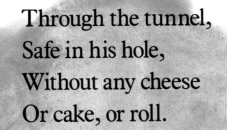

Through the tunnel,
Safe in his hole,
Without any cheese
Or cake, or roll.

15

"I'll try it again,"
He said to himself,
As he made his way
To the cupboard shelf.

Through the tunnel,
Over the bridge,
Up the mountain
By the fridge.

Into the cupboard
To look all around,
He smelled something good
And quickly found ...

a note!

"Dear Little Mouse,
Mom set the trap
But I left a treat.
Follow the map."

Out of the kitchen,
Down the hall,
To the boy's bedroom,
No trouble at all.

There was the treat
Just as he read,
In a new cage,
By the little boy's bed.

Into the cage
To look all around,
He smelled something good
And quickly found ...

a piece of cheese ...

22

and a friend!

A safe place to eat.
At last, no more trail.
A happy ending
To a mouse's tale.